City Cat

Written by Tony Langham
Illustrated by Lynne Willey

Heinemann

Chapter 1

Tabitha was a travelling cat. She was always on the move. She was always looking for new places to go and new people to see.

One day Tabitha got on a plane without anyone seeing her and went all the way to America.

The first thing Tabitha saw when she
got to America was a big sign.
It said, 'Welcome to New York'.
Tabitha wondered what to do first.
There was so much to see in New York.
Off she went to look around.

New York was a very big city. It had lots of tall buildings - very tall buildings, and the streets were full of people, cars, buses and taxis. It was very noisy! Tabitha didn't know which way to go.

5

Then Tabitha saw some people going
down an escalator. She decided to
follow them. Down, down, down
she went.

At the bottom of the escalator was a platform and a long dark tunnel. Lots of people were waiting on the platform. Tabitha liked it down there because it was nice and quiet. She lay down under a seat and went to sleep.

Suddenly Tabitha woke up with a jump. There was a very loud noise and something was coming out of the tunnel. Tabitha was very scared. She didn't wait to see what was making the noise. She just ran as fast as she could back along the tunnel and up the escalator. Up, up, up she went.

Without stopping to look, Tabitha ran
out on to the street.

SCREEEEECH! A big yellow taxi
nearly ran over her.

'You stupid cat!' the driver shouted.

Tabitha went on running until she got
to the other side of the street. There
she saw a sign to a park.

It was much quieter in the park and
there was lots of green grass and lots
of flowers. Tabitha sat on a wall and
watched all the people go by.
There were people running,
people riding bicycles,
people playing music
and even people juggling.
Some people were sitting on the grass
and eating sandwiches. Suddenly
Tabitha felt very hungry.

Just then Tabitha saw a little girl.
She was sitting on a bench next to
her mother, and she had a rag doll.
The girl was eating a big sandwich.
Tabitha hoped the girl might give her
some of the sandwich.

So Tabitha went over and sat down
near the little girl. She looked up at
her with hungry eyes. The little girl
looked at Tabitha.

'Hello pussycat,' she said.

'Meow,' went Tabitha.

The little girl laughed.

'Did you hear that, Mum?' she said.

'This pussycat just said "hello".'

'That's nice, Helen,' said her mother,
but she didn't look up from her book.

Helen looked at Tabitha.

'Do you want some of my sandwich?'
she asked.

'Meow,' went Tabitha.

Helen threw Tabitha a bit of her
sandwich and Tabitha ate it up
very quickly. So Helen gave Tabitha
some more bits and Tabitha ate up
all those too. Soon all the sandwich
was gone.

Just then Helen's mother said,
'Come on, Helen. It's time to go home.'
'Do we have to?' said Helen.
But her mother was already walking
off so Helen had to follow her.
Tabitha was sad to see them go.
She liked the little girl.
But then she saw the rag doll. Helen
had left it on the bench. Tabitha
jumped up, picked up the doll in her
mouth and ran off after the little girl.

Chapter 2

When Tabitha got to the park gates,
she saw Helen and her mother getting
on to a bus. She quickly ran after them.
She jumped on to a car and then on to
the roof of the bus. It started to move
off down the street.

Tabitha liked riding
on the roof of the bus.
It was a much nicer
way to see New York.

Inside the bus Helen suddenly said,
'Oh no! I've left my rag doll in the
park,' and she started to cry.
'Don't worry,' said her mother, 'we can
get you another one.'
But that didn't make Helen feel
any better.

Soon the bus stopped and Helen and
her mother got off and walked down
the street. Tabitha jumped down
from the roof of the bus and ran
after them. She saw them climb up
some steps and go into a tall house.
Tabitha stopped. She wondered how
she could get into the house.

Tabitha walked to
the end of the street
and went round the
backs of the houses.
She found Helen's
house and climbed
up the fire escape.

She looked in
the first window.
Helen was
not there.

Then she looked in
the next window.
There was Helen.

Helen was sitting on her bed. She looked very sad.

'Meow,' went Tabitha as loudly as she could.

Helen turned round. She couldn't believe her eyes. She opened the window and Tabitha jumped down on to the bed and gave Helen the rag doll.

'Oh thank you,' said Helen. 'What a clever pussycat you are!'

21

Just then Helen's mother came into
the room. She saw Helen holding
the rag doll.
'How did you get your rag doll back?'
she asked Helen.
'The pussycat from the park followed
us home. She gave it to me.'
'What cat?' asked Helen's mother.

'That one,' said Helen.

But when she turned round, Tabitha
was not there.

Tabitha was already back in the street riding on the roof of a taxi – a big yellow New York taxi. She was off on her travels again. She never stayed in one place for long because Tabitha was a travelling cat.